Leave It to the Molesons!

Leave It to the
Molesons!

Stories by **Burny Bos**
Pictures by **Hans de Beer**

Translated by J. Alison James

North-South Books
New York / London

First published in the United States, Great Britain, Canada,
Australia, and New Zealand in 1995 by North-South Books,
an imprint of Nord-Süd Verlag AG, Gossau Zürich, Switzerland.

Distributed in the United States by North-South Books Inc., New York.

Library of Congress Cataloging-in-Publication Data is available.
A CIP catalogue record for this book is available from The British Library.
ISBN 1-55858-431-5 (TRADE BINDING)
1 3 5 7 9 TB 10 8 6 4 2
ISBN 1-55858-432-3 (LIBRARY BINDING)
1 3 5 7 9 LB 10 8 6 4 2
Printed in Belgium

Contents

Meet the Molesons

Let me introduce you to my family.
That's my mother, Molly, up there, with
my father. His is name Morris—Mud, for
short. He works around the house, while
she slaves away at the office. Dusty, my
twin sister, and I go to school. We play
with Grandma, who is pretty wild for an
old lady. And my name is Dug (short for
Dugless). There's nothing special about us,
except sometimes we do stuff that's funny.
Your family does too, I'm sure. You should
write a book about it. For now, you can
read mine and have a few laughs.

Dish Washing Made Easy

One hot summer day not long ago, we had a party. Lots of people came to our house for lunch. When they finally left, there was a mountain of dishes in the kitchen.

Mother and Father were wrung out like wet towels. They flopped on the sofa.

"If only we didn't have to clean up," moaned Mother.

Then Dusty got an inspired idea. She whispered it in my ear. Then she said sweetly, "Mother, Father, why don't you take a nap while Dug and I do the dishes?"

"What a great idea," said Father. "I should have thought of it myself."

"Are you feeling all right?" Mother asked us.

Dusty and I laughed. As soon as they were out of sight, we carried the dishes outside.

Dusty pointed the hose at the pile.
"Ready? Aim! Fire!" she shouted. I turned
on the water full blast and held the dishes
up like targets. Dusty sprayed. I got
soaked. It felt great!

"Your turn!" I shouted. Soon the dishes
were spotless and shining in the hot sun.

We didn't hear the door open and
Mother come out. She cried, "What do
you think you are—"

SPLAAALPFFF! I turned around and accidentally sprayed her right in the face. Uh-oh, I thought. Trouble.

Mother said, "Give me that hose!"

Just then Father came outside, rubbing
his eyes. "What's going on—AAARGH!"
Mother sprayed him with the hose.

"We've invented an automatic
dish-washing machine," Dusty shouted.

"Hand me the hose," Father said. "I see
a spot on this plate." He sprayed all three
of us until we were dripping wet.

Dish washing was never so much fun.

Wallpapering Is Child's Play

One Saturday my parents decided
to wallpaper the living room. We took
all the furniture out and put in a long
wallpaper table. "Should we look at the
instructions?" Mother asked.

Father laughed. "Don't be silly," he said.
"Wallpapering is child's play. Cut, paste,
stick. If everyone helps, we'll be done
before noon."

Mother cut the first sheet of paper.
Father loaded up a brush with wallpaper
paste. "Dusty, hold that end flat," he said.
But Dusty let go too soon, and the paper
rolled back like a spring. SNAP, it hit
Father on the nose, and the dripping brush
went flying.

"Why don't you two children work together?" Mother suggested. Father gave us a sheet of paper wet with paste.

Dusty said, "I'll hold it up while you stick it on the wall." But somehow Dusty got stuck on the wall too. "LED ME OUD OB HERE!" Dusty cried.

"Can someone give me a hand?" called Mother. "I can't quite reach the ceiling."

"Here, let me," said Father. He stepped up on a chair, and then turned and reached for the paper. "Ow ow ow oooh!" he cried. We all looked at him in surprise.

"What's the matter, dear?" asked Mother.

"My back," moaned Father. "I can't stand up."

"Oh, for heaven's sake," said Mother. Then she had an idea. "Just stay there a moment, will you dear?" She lifted Dusty up to stand on Father's back.

"What on earth?" cried Father.

"Just for a second, sweetheart," said Mother. She handed Dusty the brush, and in a flash Dusty stuck the wallpaper up in the right spot.

Then Mother helped Father down from the chair.

Luckily Father's back felt better after a few minutes, and we could get back to work. Pretty soon we got the hang of it, and we finished the entire living room before midnight!

The Tree House

One afternoon Dusty and I decided to build ourselves a tree house in the big oak tree behind the house. "Let's do it all by ourselves," I said.

"I'll get the wood," said Dusty.

We soon ran out of nails.

"Father," I called. "We need more nails!"

He looked at our work. "Don't you think that board is a little long?" he said. "Let me cut off a piece." Pretty soon he was hammering nails and whistling,

completely absorbed in building our tree house.

"Stay out of the way!" he warned us.

Dusty and I got sick of watching. We went inside and turned on the TV.

Then Mother came home. "What are
you two doing watching TV on such a
beautiful day?" she scolded.

"We wanted to build a tree house," I
explained.

And Dusty said, "But Father thought he
could do it better."

Mother stormed outside. We followed.

"Isn't this a fabulous tree house!" called Father from up in the tree. "I haven't had so much fun since I was a boy!"

Mother lost her angry look. "It's lovely, sweetheart. May we come up for a visit?"

"It's not quite finished," said Father.

We scrambled up the ladder anyway.

It was very sturdy. Father was so proud.
Mother made us lemonade while we
hammered in the last few nails. While we
had our drinks, Father told us about the
tree houses he built when he was young.
Later on, Dusty and I drew plans for some
furniture. "This time we'll do it ourselves,"
I promised. "When Father isn't home!"

The Scream

One day, when we got home from school, Mother was frantically trying to get off a few business letters.

"I'll take the children to the museum so you can have some peace and quiet," Father said. "It's important for their education."

Dusty and I smiled. We loved to see the dinosaurs, and the stuffed bears and wolves.

But this time we went to a museum of modern art. At the entrance, Father whispered, "This is a place of *culture*. Be quiet and don't touch a thing."

"These paintings are wired to an alarm system to prevent cat burglars from stealing them," he explained.

"Cool!" I cried.

"Shhh!" whispered Dusty.

We looked at a huge orange painting with a yellow and blue stripe. "Now this is *art*," said Father. "Isn't it peaceful?" He read the label, "'1967, oil on canvas.'" Then he showed us what to do. "To see it properly, screw up your eyes a little."

We screwed up our eyes. The painting looked the same, just a little blurry.

"You get a better perspective if you look at it from a distance," he explained. He squinted at the painting and walked back further and further, until—CRASH! He banged right into another painting!

The alarm started screaming like two cats in a fight. A guard stormed into the room and grabbed Father.

"It was only a mistake!" Father stammered. "Do I look like a cat burglar? Look, these are my two children." Why did he have to bring us into it!

"Well, how was the museum?" asked Mother when we got home.

"It was great," Dusty said. "We liked the picture that screamed the best."

"'The Scream?'" asked Mother, surprised. "At our museum?"

She looked at Father.

"Not exactly. You see, there was this little problem— Hey, isn't that the bell for the ice-cream man?"

We ran outside. Father bought an ice-cream cone for each of us. We usually have to share. They were delicious. So delicious that we forgot all about the screaming picture.

Soaked to the Skin

It was raining.

It had been raining all morning.

There was nothing to do.

Father looked out of the window and said, "Am I ever glad to be warm and dry indoors. Just look at that rain!"

That gave me an idea.

"Can we go outside to play?"

"Yes! Yes, please!" cried Dusty.

"Are you crazy? You'd get soaked."

"We'll wear raincoats," I said.

"And boots," said Dusty.

It was great. We jumped in the puddles. We tried to make the water splash up inside the umbrella.

"This is as good as jumping in piles of leaves," Dusty said.

"Do you think if we jumped from the
wall, we could make a bigger splash?" I
asked her.

Dusty scrambled up and jumped.

Then it was my turn. But my boots were
slippery, and I fell off the wall. I landed on

the umbrella, and it flipped up and poked me in the head. I started to cry.

Father saw everything. He came running. But he came so fast, he forgot to put on his raincoat.

He even forgot his boots.

He was soaked to the skin.

He picked me up and carried me inside. I was fine. Inside my raincoat I was as dry as a bone. My bump had even stopped hurting. Father stood in the doorway and dripped. "Ah-ah-ah—*TCHOOO!*" he sneezed.

Dusty and I bundled Father up in a blanket by the fire. We put his feet to soak in warm water. "Thank . . . ah-ah-ah-*tch*—*YOU!*" he said.

Dusty shook her head.

"You should know better than to go out without your raincoat in a storm like this," she said.

Father smiled and blew his nose.

We All Sing for Ice Cream

Grandma came back from shopping. Usually she brings us a little something. We stood around trying not to look too eager. She fished in her purse. "Oh," she said sadly, "I forgot to get something for you two. Maybe I have a piece of chocolate in my bag."

"Never mind," said Dusty.

"It's okay," I said.

Grandma didn't find a single piece of chocolate in her purse. But she did find a little card. "Look at this!" she said proudly. "This is my new plastic money. A credit card is something quite modern. You can buy simply anything with it. Without spending any real money."

"Even ice cream?" I asked.

"Of course ice cream," Grandma said.

"I don't believe you," Dusty said.

"Just you wait and see," said Grandma. "Let's go to town. I will buy a new hat and get you some ice cream. I'll show you how this thing works!"

It didn't take Grandma long to buy the hat. She just rolled in, gave them her new card, and rolled back out wearing a hat.

But it wasn't so easy to get ice cream. They said they didn't take credit cards.

"What a funny old world," said Grandma. We strolled along miserably. When we passed a music shop, Grandma had an idea. She went right in and bought a recorder. They took her card all right.

"Now we can make some real money," she said.

Dusty set Grandma's new hat upside down on the pavement. Then Grandma started to play the recorder. Some of the songs we knew, so we sang along. People stopped to listen. A few of them tossed coins into the hat. When we stopped, they clapped and threw more coins.

"That should be enough," Grandma said, smiling. "All right, children, what kind of ice cream do you want?"

"You are absolutely the best, Grandma," I said.

She nodded. She knew it.

Another Day

I wanted to tell you about the time Father tried to raise chickens. It was really funny. But my pencil is worn right down to the stub. And I've run out of paper. So you'll just have to imagine it. That won't be hard—our family is pretty ordinary. Just like yours, I'll bet. So why don't you write down a thing or two? Just for a laugh.

Burny Bos was born in Haarlem, in the Netherlands. He began his career as a teacher, and in 1973 he started developing children's shows for Dutch radio. Within a few years he was working for Dutch television as well. He currently makes records and cassette tapes for children and has won many prizes for his children's broadcasts, films, and recordings. He has also written more than twenty-five children's books, several of which have been illustrated by Hans de Beer.

He lives with his wife, two daughters, and a little son in Bussum, which is near Amsterdam.

Hans de Beer was born in 1957 in Muiden, a small town near Amsterdam, in the Netherlands. He began to draw when he went to school, mostly when the lessons got too boring. In college he studied history, but he was drawing so many pictures during the lectures that he decided to become an artist. He went on to study illustration at the Rietveld Academy of Art in Amsterdam.

Hans de Beer's first book, *Little Polar Bear*, was very popular around the world. The book has been published in eighteen languages. Hans had so much fun illustrating picture books that he did more and more of them. He likes to draw polar bears, cats, walruses, elephants, and moles.

His books have received many prizes, among them the first prize from an international jury of children in Bologna, Italy.

Hans de Beer now lives in Amsterdam with his wife, who is also a children's book illustrator.

North-South Easy-to-Read Books

Rinaldo, the Sly Fox
by Ursel Scheffler, illustrated by Iskender Gider

The Return of Rinaldo, the Sly Fox
by Ursel Scheffler, illustrated by Iskender Gider

Rinaldo on the Run
by Ursel Scheffler, illustrated by Iskender Gider

Loretta and the Little Fairy
by Gerda Marie Scheidl, illustrated by Christa Unzner-Fischer

Little Polar Bear and the Brave Little Hare
by Hans de Beer

Where's Molly?
by Uli Waas

The Extraordinary Adventures of an Ordinary Hat
by Wolfram Hänel, illustrated by Christa Unzner-Fischer

Mia the Beach Cat
by Wolfram Hänel, illustrated by Kirsten Höecker

The Old Man and the Bear
by Wolfram Hänel, illustrated by Jean-Pierre Corderoc'h

Lila's Little Dinosaur
by Wolfram Hänel, illustrated by Alex de Wolf

Meet the Molesons
by Burny Bos, illustrated by Hans de Beer

More from the Molesons
by Burny Bos, illustrated by Hans de Beer

On the Road with Poppa Whopper
by Marianne Busser and Ron Schröder,
illustrated by Hans de Beer

Spiny
by Jürgen Lassig, illustrated by Uli Waas